IN THE
WALLS OF ERYX

Fantasy & Horror Classics

By

H. P. LOVECRAFT

WITH A
DEDICATION BY
GEORGE HENRY WEISS

First published in 1939

To
HOWARD PHILLIPS LOVECRAFT

Essayist, Poet &
Master-writer of the Weird
1890-1937

He lived—and now is dead beyond all knowing
Of life and death: the vast and formless scheme
Behind the face of nature ever showing
Has swallowed up the dreamer and the dream.
But brief the hour he had upon the stream
Of timeless time from past to future flowing
To lift his sail and catch the luminous gleam
Of stars that marked his coming and his going
Before he vanished: yet the brilliant wake
His passing left is vivid on the tide
And for the countless centuries will abide:
The genius that no death can ever take
Crowns him immortal, though a man has died.

FRANCIS FLAGG
(*George Henry Weiss*)

CONTENTS

H. P. Lovecraft

Howard Phillips Lovecraft was born in 1890 in Rhode Island, USA. Although a sickly boy, Lovecraft began writing at a very young age, quickly developing a deep and abiding interest in science. At just sixteen he was writing a monthly astronomy column for his local newspaper. However, in 1908, Lovecraft suffered a nervous breakdown and failed to get into university, sparking a period of five years in which he all but vanished.

In 1913, Lovecraft was invited to join the UAPA (United Amateur Press Association)—a development which re-invigorated his writing. In 1917, he began to focus on fiction, producing such well-known early stories as *Dagon* and *A Reminiscence of Dr. Samuel Johnson*. In 1924, Lovecraft married and moved to New York, but he disliked life there intensely, and struggled to find work. A few years later, penniless and now divorced, he returned to Rhode Island. It was here, during the last decade of his life, that Lovecraft produced the vast majority of his best-known fiction, including *The Dunwich Horror*, *The Shadow over Innsmouth*, *The Thing on the Doorstep* and arguably his most famous story, *The Call of Cthulhu*. Having suffered from cancer of the small intestine for more than a year, Lovecraft died in March of 1937.

IN THE WALLS OF ERYX

Before I try to rest I will set down these notes in preparation for the report I must make. What I have found is so singular, and so contrary to all past experience and expectations, that it deserves a very careful description.

I reached the main landing on Venus March 18, terrestrial time; VI, 9 of the planet's calendar. Being put in the main group under Miller, I received my equipment—watch tuned to Venus's slightly quicker rotation—and went through the usual mask drill. After two days I was pronounced fit for duty.

Leaving the Crystal Company's post at Terra Nova around dawn, VI, 12, I followed the southerly route which Anderson had mapped out from the air. The going was bad, for these jungles are always half impassable after a rain. It must be the moisture that gives the tangled vines and creepers that leathery toughness; a toughness so great that a knife has to work ten minutes on some of them. By noon it was dryer—the vegetation getting soft and rubbery so that the knife went through it easily—but even then I could not make much speed. These Carter oxygen masks are too heavy—just carrying one half wears an ordinary man out. A Dubois mask with sponge-reservoir instead of tubes would give just as good air at half the weight.

The crystal-detector seemed to function well, pointing steadily in a direction verifying Anderson's report. It is curious how that principle of affinity works—without any of the fakery of the old 'divining rods' back home. There must be a great deposit of crystals within a thousand miles, though I suppose those damnable man-lizards always watch and guard it. Possibly they think we are just as foolish for coming to Venus to hunt the stuff as we think they are for grovelling in the mud whenever they see a piece of it, or for keeping that great mass on a pedestal in their temple. I wish they'd get a new religion, for they have no use for the crystals except to pray to. Barring theology, they would let us take all we want—and even if they learned to tap them for power there'd be more than enough for their planet and the earth besides. I for one am tired of passing up the main deposits and merely seeking separate crystals out of jungle river-beds. Sometime I'll urge the wiping out of these scaly beggars by a good stiff army from home. About twenty ships could bring enough troops across to turn the trick. One can't call the damned things men for all their "cities" and towers. They haven't any skill except building— and using swords and poison darts—and I don't believe their so-called "cities" mean much more than ant-hills or beaver-dams. I doubt if they even have a real language—all the talk about psychological communication through those tentacles down their chests strikes me as bunk. What misleads people is their upright posture; just an accidental physical resemblance to terrestrial man.

I'd like to go through a Venus jungle for once without having to watch out for skulking groups of them or dodge their cursed darts. They may have been all right before we began to take the crystals, but they're certainly a bad enough nuisance now— with their dart-shooting and their cutting of our water pipes. More and more I come to believe that they have a special sense like our crystal-detectors. No one ever knew them to bother a man—apart from long-distance sniping—who didn't have crystals on him.

Around 1 p.m. a dart nearly took my helmet off, and I thought for a second one of my oxygen tubes was punctured. The sly devils hadn't made a sound, but three of them were closing in on me. I got them all by sweeping in a circle with my flame pistol, for even though their colour blended with the jungle, I could spot the moving creepers. One of them was fully eight feet tall, with a snout like a tapir's. The other two were average seven-footers. All that makes them hold their own is sheer numbers—even a single regiment of flame throwers could raise hell with them. It is curious, though, how they've come to be dominant on the planet. Not another living thing higher than the wriggling akmans and skorahs, or the flying tukahs of the other continent—unless of course those holes in the Dionaean Plateau hide something.

About two o'clock my detector veered westward, indicating isolated crystals ahead on the right. This checked up with Anderson, and I turned my course accordingly. It was harder going—not only because the ground was rising, but because the animal life and carnivorous plants were thicker. I was always slashing ugrats and stepping on skorahs, and my leather suit was all speckled from the bursting darohs which struck it from all sides. The sunlight was all the worse because of the mist, and did not seem to dry up the mud in the least. Every time I stepped my feet sank down five or six inches, and there was a sucking sort of blup every time I pulled them out. I wish somebody would invent a safe kind of suiting other than leather for this climate. Cloth of course would rot; but some thin metallic tissue that couldn't tear—like the surface of this revolving decay-proof record scroll—ought to be feasible some time.

I ate about 3:30—if slipping these wretched food tablets through my mask can be called eating. Soon after that I noticed a decided change in the landscape—the bright, poisonous-looking flowers shifting in colour and getting wraith-like. The outlines of everything shimmered rhythmically, and bright points of light appeared and danced in the same slow, steady tempo. After that the temperature seemed to fluctuate in unison with a peculiar rhythmic drumming.

The whole universe seemed to be throbbing in deep, regular pulsations that filled every corner of space and flowed through my body and mind alike. I lost all sense of equilibrium and staggered dizzily, nor did it change things in the least when I shut my eyes and covered my ears with my hands. However, my mind was still clear, and in a very few minutes I realised what had happened.

I had encountered at last one of those curious mirage-plants about which so many of our men told stories. Anderson had warned me of them, and described their appearance very closely—the shaggy stalk, the spiky leaves, and the mottled blossoms whose gaseous, dream-breeding exhalations penetrate every existing make of mask.

Recalling what happened to Bailey three years ago, I fell into a momentary panic, and began to dash and stagger about in the crazy, chaotic world which the plant's exhalations had woven around me. Then good sense came back, and I realised all I need do was retreat from the dangerous blossoms; heading away from the source of the pulsations, and cutting a path blindly—regardless of what might seem to swirl around me—until safely out of the plant's effective radius.

Although everything was spinning perilously, I tried to start in the right direction and hack my way ahead. My route must have been far from straight, for it seemed hours before I was free of the mirage-plant's pervasive influence. Gradually the dancing lights began to disappear, and the shimmering spectral scenery began to assume the aspect of solidity. When I did get wholly clear I looked at my watch and was astonished to find that the time was only 4:20. Though eternities had seemed to pass, the whole experience could have consumed little more than a half-hour.

Every delay, however, was irksome, and I had lost ground in my retreat from the plant. I now pushed ahead in the uphill direction indicated by the crystal-detector, bending every energy toward making better time. The jungle was still thick, though there was less animal life. Once a carnivorous blossom engulfed my right foot and held it so tightly that I had to hack it free with my knife; reducing the flower to strips before it let go.

In less than an hour I saw that the jungle growths were thinning out, and by five o'clock—after passing through a belt of tree-ferns with very little underbrush—I emerged on a broad mossy plateau. My progress now became rapid, and I saw by the wavering of my detector-needle that I was getting relatively close to the crystal I sought. This was odd, for most of the scattered, egg-like spheroids occurred in jungle streams of a sort not likely to be found on this treeless upland.

The terrain sloped upward, ending in a definite crest. I reached the top about 5:30, and saw ahead of me a very extensive plain with forests in the distance. This, without question, was the plateau mapped by Matsugawa from the air fifty years ago, and called on our maps "Eryx" or the "Erycinian Highland." But what made my heart leap was a smaller detail, whose position could not have been far from the plain's exact centre. It was a single point of light, blazing through the mist and seeming to draw a piercing, concentrated luminescence from the yellowish, vapour-dulled sunbeams. This, without doubt, was the crystal I sought—a thing possibly no larger than a hen's egg, yet containing enough power to keep a city warm for a year. I could hardly wonder, as I glimpsed the distant glow, that those miserable man-lizards worship such crystals. And yet they have not the least notion of the powers they contain.

Breaking into a rapid run, I tried to reach the unexpected prize as soon as possible; and was annoyed when the firm moss gave place to a thin, singularly detestable mud studded with occasional patches of weeds and creepers. But I splashed on heedlessly—scarcely thinking to look around for any of the skulking man-lizards. In this open space I was not very likely to be waylaid. As I advanced, the light ahead seemed to grow in size and brilliancy, and I began to notice some peculiarity in its situation. Clearly, this was a crystal of the very finest quality, and my elation grew with every spattering step.

It is now that I must begin to be careful in making my report, since what I shall henceforward have to say involves unprecedented—though fortunately verifiable—matters. I was racing ahead with mounting eagerness, and had come within an hundred yards or so of the crystal—whose position on a sort of raised place in the omnipresent slime seemed very odd—when a sudden, overpowering force struck my chest and the knuckles of my clenched fists and knocked me over backward into the mud. The splash of my fall was terrific, nor did the softness of the ground and the presence of some slimy weeds and creepers save my head from a bewildering jarring. For a moment I lay supine, too utterly startled to think. Then I half-mechanically stumbled to my feet and began to scrape the worst of the mud and scum from my leather suit.

Of what I had encountered I could not form the faintest idea. I had seen nothing which could have caused the shock, and I saw nothing now. Had I, after all, merely slipped in the mud? My sore knuckles and aching chest forbade me to think so. Or was this whole incident an illusion brought on by some hidden mirage-plant? It hardly seemed probable, since I had none of the usual symptoms, and since there was no place near by where so vivid and typical a growth could lurk unseen. Had I been on the earth, I would have suspected a barrier of N-force laid down by some government to mark a forbidden zone, but in this humanless region such a notion would have been absurd.

Finally pulling myself together, I decided to investigate in a cautious way. Holding my knife as far as possible ahead of me, so that it might be first to feel the strange force, I started once more for the shining crystal—preparing to advance step by step with the greatest deliberation. At the third step I was brought up short by the impact of the knife-point on an apparently solid surface—a solid surface where my eyes saw nothing.

After a moment's recoil I gained boldness. Extending my gloved left hand, I verified the presence of invisible solid matter— or a tactile illusion of solid matter—ahead of me. Upon moving my hand I found that the barrier was of substantial extent, and of an almost glassy smoothness, with no evidence of the joining of separate blocks. Nerving myself for further experiments, I removed a glove and tested the thing with my bare hand. It was indeed hard and glassy, and of a curious coldness as contrasted with the air around. I strained my eyesight to the utmost in an effort to glimpse some trace of the obstructing substance, but could discern nothing whatsoever. There was not even any evidence of refractive power as judged by the aspect of the landscape ahead. Absence of reflective power was proved by the lack of a glowing image of the sun at any point.

Burning curiosity began to displace all other feelings, and I enlarged my investigations as best I could. Exploring with my hands, I found that the barrier extended from the ground to some level higher than I could reach, and that it stretched off indefinitely on both sides. It was, then, a wall of some kind— though all guesses as to its materials and its purpose were beyond me. Again I thought of the mirage-plant and the dreams it induced, but a moment's reasoning put this out of my head.

Knocking sharply on the barrier with the hilt of my knife, and kicking at it with my heavy boots, I tried to interpret the sounds thus made. There was something suggestive of cement or concrete in these reverberations, though my hands had found the surface more glassy or metallic in feel. Certainly, I was confronting something strange beyond all previous experience.

The next logical move was to get some idea of the wall's dimensions. The height problem would be hard if not insoluble, but the length and shape problem could perhaps be sooner dealt with. Stretching out my arms and pressing close to the barrier, I began to edge gradually to the left—keeping very careful track of the way I faced. After several steps I concluded that the wall was not straight, but that I was following part of some vast circle or ellipse. And then my attention was distracted by something wholly different—something connected with the still-distant crystal which had formed the object of my quest.

I have said that even from a greater distance the shining object's position seemed indefinably queer—on a slight mound rising from the slime. Now—at about an hundred yards—I could see plainly despite the engulfing mist just what that mound was. It was the body of a man in one of the Crystal Company's leather suits, lying on his back, and with his oxygen mask half buried in the mud a few inches away. In his right hand, crushed convulsively against his chest, was the crystal which had led me here—a spheroid of incredible size, so large that the dead fingers could scarcely close over it. Even at the given distance I could see that the body was a recent one. There was little visible decay, and I reflected that in this climate such a thing meant death not more than a day before. Soon the hateful farnoth-flies would begin to cluster about the corpse. I wondered who the man was. Surely no one I had seen on this trip. It must have been one of the old-timers absent on a long roving commission, who had come to this especial region independently of Anderson's survey. There he lay, past all trouble, and with the rays of the great crystal streaming out from between his stiffened fingers.

For fully five minutes I stood there staring in bewilderment and apprehension. A curious dread assailed me, and I had an unreasonable impulse to run away. It could not have been done by those slinking man-lizards, for he still held the crystal he had found. Was there any connexion with the invisible wall? Where had he found the crystal? Anderson's instrument had indicated one in this quarter well before this man could have perished. I now began to regard the unseen barrier as something sinister, and recoiled from it with a shudder. Yet I knew I must probe the mystery all the more quickly and thoroughly because of this recent tragedy.

Suddenly—wrenching my mind back to the problem I faced—I thought of a possible means of testing the wall's height, or at least of finding whether or not it extended indefinitely upward. Seizing a handful of mud, I let it drain until it gained some coherence and then flung it high in the air toward the utterly transparent barrier. At a height of perhaps fourteen feet it struck the invisible surface with a resounding splash, disintegrating at once and oozing downward in disappearing streams with surprising rapidity. Plainly, the wall was a lofty one. A second handful, hurled at an even sharper angle, hit the surface about eighteen feet from the ground and disappeared as quickly as the first.

I now summoned up all my strength and prepared to throw a third handful as high as I possibly could. Letting the mud drain, and squeezing it to maximum dryness, I flung it up so steeply that I feared it might not reach the obstructing surface at all. It did, however, and this time it crossed the barrier and fell in the mud beyond with a violent spattering. At last I had a rough idea of the height of the wall, for the crossing had evidently occurred some twenty or 21 feet aloft.

With a nineteen- or twenty-foot vertical wall of glassy flatness, ascent was clearly impossible. I must, then, continue to circle the barrier in the hope of finding a gate, an ending, or some sort of interruption. Did the obstacle form a complete round or other closed figure, or was it merely an arc or semicircle? Acting on my decision, I resumed my slow leftward circling, moving my hands up and down over the unseen surface on the chance of finding some window or other small aperture. Before starting, I tried to mark my position by kicking a hole in the mud, but found the slime too thin to hold any impression. I did, though, gauge the place approximately by noting a tall cycad in the distant forest which seemed just on a line with the gleaming crystal an hundred yards away. If no gate or break existed I could now tell when I had completely circumnavigated the wall.

I had not progressed far before I decided that the curvature indicated a circular enclosure of about an hundred yards' diameter—provided the outline was regular. This would mean that the dead man lay near the wall at a point almost opposite the region where I had started. Was he just inside or just outside the enclosure? This I would soon ascertain.

As I slowly rounded the barrier without finding any gate, window, or other break, I decided that the body was lying within. On closer view, the features of the dead man seemed vaguely disturbing. I found something alarming in his expression, and in the way the glassy eyes stared. By the time I was very near I believed I recognised him as Dwight, a veteran whom I had never known, but who was pointed out to me at the post last year. The crystal he clutched was certainly a prize—the largest single specimen I had ever seen.

I was so near the body that I could—but for the barrier—have touched it, when my exploring left hand encountered a corner in the unseen surface. In a second I had learned that there was an opening about three feet wide, extending from the ground to a height greater than I could reach. There was no door, nor any evidence of hinge-marks bespeaking a former door. Without a moment's hesitation I stepped through and advanced two paces to the prostrate body—which lay at right angles to the hallway I had entered, in what seemed to be an intersecting doorless corridor. It gave me a fresh curiosity to find that the interior of this vast enclosure was divided by partitions.

Bending to examine the corpse, I discovered that it bore no wounds. This scarcely surprised me, since the continued presence of the crystal argued against the pseudo-reptilian natives. Looking about for some possible cause of death, my eyes lit upon the oxygen mask lying close to the body's feet. Here, indeed, was something significant. Without this device no human being could breathe the air of Venus for more than thirty seconds, and Dwight—if it were he—had obviously lost his. Probably it had been carelessly buckled, so that the weight of the tubes worked the straps loose—a thing which could not happen with a Dubois sponge-reservoir mask. The half-minute of grace had been too short to allow the man to stoop and recover his protection—or else the cyanogen content of the atmosphere was abnormally high at the time. Probably he had been busy admiring the crystal—wherever he may have found it. He had, apparently, just taken it from the pouch in his suit, for the flap was unbuttoned.

I now proceeded to extricate the huge crystal from the dead prospector's fingers—a task which the body's stiffness made very difficult. The spheroid was larger than a man's fist, and glowed as if alive in the reddish rays of the westering sun. As I touched the gleaming surface I shuddered involuntarily—as if by taking this precious object I had transferred to myself the doom which had overtaken its earlier bearer. However, my qualms soon passed, and I carefully buttoned the crystal into the pouch of my leather suit. Superstition has never been one of my failings.

Placing the man's helmet over his dead, staring face, I straightened up and stepped back through the unseen doorway to the entrance hall of the great enclosure. All my curiosity about the strange edifice now returned, and I racked my brain with speculations regarding its material, origin, and purpose. That the hands of men had reared it I could not for a moment believe. Our ships first reached Venus only 72 years ago, and the only human beings on the planet have been those at Terra Nova. Nor does human knowledge include any perfectly transparent, non-refractive solid such as the substance of this building. Prehistoric human invasions of Venus can be pretty well ruled out, so that one must turn to the idea of native construction. Did a forgotten race of highly evolved beings precede the man-lizards as masters of Venus? Despite their elaborately built cities, it seemed hard to credit the pseudo-reptiles with anything of this kind. There must have been another race aeons ago, of which this is perhaps the last relique. Or will other ruins of kindred origin be found by future expeditions? The purpose of such a structure passes all conjecture—but its strange and seemingly non-practical material suggests a religious use.

Realising my inability to solve these problems, I decided that all I could do was to explore the invisible structure itself. That various rooms and corridors extended over the seemingly unbroken plain of mud I felt convinced; and I believed that a knowledge of their plan might lead to something significant. So, feeling my way back through the doorway and edging past the body, I began to advance along the corridor toward those interior regions whence the dead man had presumably come.

Later on I would investigate the hallway I had left.

Groping like a blind man despite the misty sunlight, I moved slowly onward. Soon the corridor turned sharply and began to spiral in toward the centre in ever-diminishing curves. Now and then my touch would reveal a doorless intersecting passage, and I several times encountered junctions with two, three, or four diverging avenues. In these latter cases I always followed the inmost route, which seemed to form a continuation of the one I had been traversing. There would be plenty of time to examine the branches after I had reached and returned from the main regions. I can scarcely describe the strangeness of the experience—threading the unseen ways of an invisible structure reared by forgotten hands on an alien planet!

At last, still stumbling and groping, I felt the corridor end in a sizeable open space. Fumbling about, I found I was in a circular chamber about ten feet across; and from the position of the dead man against certain distant forest landmarks I judged that this chamber lay at or near the centre of the edifice. Out of it opened five corridors besides the one through which I had entered, but I kept the latter in mind by sighting very carefully past the body to a particular tree on the horizon as I stood just within the entrance.

There was nothing in this room to distinguish it—merely the floor of thin mud which was everywhere present. Wondering whether this part of the building had any roof, I repeated my experiment with an upward-flung handful of mud, and found at once that no covering existed. If there had ever been one, it must have fallen long ago, for not a trace of debris or scattered blocks ever halted my feet. As I reflected, it struck me as distinctly odd that this apparently primordial structure should be so devoid of tumbling masonry, gaps in the walls, and other common attributes of dilapidation.

What was it? What had it ever been? Of what was it made? Why was there no evidence of separate blocks in the glassy, bafflingly homogeneous walls? Why were there no traces of doors, either interior or exterior? I knew only that I was in a round, roofless, doorless edifice of some hard, smooth, perfectly transparent, non-refractive, and non-reflective material, an hundred yards in diameter, with many corridors, and with a small circular room at the centre. More than this I could never learn from a direct investigation.

I now observed that the sun was sinking very low in the west—a golden-ruddy disc floating in a pool of scarlet and orange above the mist-clouded trees of the horizon. Plainly, I would have to hurry if I expected to choose a sleeping-spot on dry ground before dark. I had long before decided to camp for the night on the firm, mossy rim of the plateau near the crest whence I had first spied the shining crystal, trusting to my usual luck to save me from an attack by the man-lizards. It has always been my contention that we ought to travel in parties of two or more, so that someone can be on guard during sleeping hours, but the really small number of night attacks makes the Company careless about such things. Those scaly wretches seem to have difficulty in seeing at night, even with curious glow-torches.

Having picked out again the hallway through which I had come, I started to return to the structure's entrance. Additional exploration could wait for another day. Groping a course as best I could through the spiral corridor—with only general sense, memory, and a vague recognition of some of the ill-defined weed patches on the plain as guides—I soon found myself once more in close proximity to the corpse. There were now one or two farnoth-flies swooping over the helmet-covered face, and I knew that decay was setting in. With a futile instinctive loathing I raised my hand to brush away this vanguard of the scavengers—when a strange and astonishing thing became manifest. An invisible wall, checking the sweep of my arm, told me that—notwithstanding my careful retracing of the way—I had not indeed returned to the corridor in which the body lay. Instead, I was in a parallel hallway, having no doubt taken some wrong turn or fork among the intricate passages behind.

Hoping to find a doorway to the exit hall ahead, I continued my advance, but presently came to a blank wall. I would, then, have to return to the central chamber and steer my course anew. Exactly where I had made my mistake I could not tell. I glanced at the ground to see if by any miracle guiding footprints had remained, but at once realised that the thin mud held impressions only for a very few moments. There was little difficulty in finding my way to the centre again, and once there I carefully reflected on the proper outward course. I had kept too far to the right before. This time I must take a more leftward fork somewhere—just where, I could decide as I went.

As I groped ahead a second time I felt quite confident of my correctness, and diverged to the left at a junction I was sure I remembered. The spiralling continued, and I was careful not to stray into any intersecting passages. Soon, however, I saw to my disgust that I was passing the body at a considerable distance; this passage evidently reached the outer wall at a point much beyond it. In the hope that another exit might exist in the half of the wall I had not yet explored, I pressed forward for several paces, but eventually came once more to a solid barrier. Clearly, the plan of the building was even more complicated than I had thought.

I now debated whether to return to the centre again or whether to try some of the lateral corridors extending toward the body. If I chose this second alternative, I would run the risk of breaking my mental pattern of where I was; hence I had better not attempt it unless I could think of some way of leaving a visible trail behind me. Just how to leave a trail would be quite a problem, and I ransacked my mind for a solution. There seemed to be nothing about my person which could leave a mark on anything, nor any material which I could scatter—or minutely subdivide and scatter.

My pen had no effect on the invisible wall, and I could not lay a trail of my precious food tablets. Even had I been willing to spare the latter, there would not have been even nearly enough—

besides which the small pellets would have instantly sunk from sight in the thin mud. I searched my pockets for an old-fashioned notebook—often used unofficially on Venus despite the quick rotting-rate of paper in the planet's atmosphere—whose pages I could tear up and scatter, but could find none. It was obviously impossible to tear the tough, thin metal of this revolving decay-proof record scroll, nor did my clothing offer any possibilities. In Venus's peculiar atmosphere I could not safely spare my stout leather suit, and underwear had been eliminated because of the climate.

I tried to smear mud on the smooth, invisible walls after squeezing it as dry as possible, but found that it slipped from sight as quickly as did the height-testing handfuls I had previously thrown. Finally I drew out my knife and attempted to scratch a line on the glassy, phantom surface—something I could recognise with my hand, even though I would not have the advantage of seeing it from afar. It was useless, however, for the blade made not the slightest impression on the baffling, unknown material.

Frustrated in all attempts to blaze a trail, I again sought the round central chamber through memory. It seemed easier to get back to this room than to steer a definite, predetermined course away from it, and I had little difficulty in finding it anew. This time I listed on my record scroll every turn I made—drawing a crude hypothetical diagram of my route, and marking all diverging corridors. It was, of course, maddeningly slow work when everything had to be determined by touch, and the possibilities of error were infinite; but I believed it would pay in the long run.

The long twilight of Venus was thick when I reached the central room, but I still had hopes of gaining the outside before dark. Comparing my fresh diagram with previous recollections, I believed I had located my original mistake, so once more set out confidently along the invisible hallways. I veered further to the left than during my previous attempts, and tried to keep track of my turnings on the record scroll in case I was still mistaken. In the gathering dusk I could see the dim line of the corpse, now the centre of a loathsome cloud of farnoth-flies. Before long, no doubt, the mud-dwelling sificlighs would be oozing in from the plain to complete the ghastly work. Approaching the body with some reluctance, I was preparing to step past it when a sudden collision with a wall told me I was again astray.

I now realised plainly that I was lost. The complications of this building were too much for offhand solution, and I would probably have to do some careful checking before I could hope to emerge. Still, I was eager to get to dry ground before total darkness set in; hence I returned once more to the centre and began a rather aimless series of trials and errors—making notes by the light of my electric lamp. When I used this device I noticed with interest that it produced no reflection—not even the faintest glistening—in the transparent walls around me. I was, however, prepared for this; since the sun had at no time formed a gleaming image in the strange material.

I was still groping about when the dusk became total. A heavy mist obscured most of the stars and planets, but the earth was plainly visible as a glowing, bluish-green point in the southeast. It was just past opposition, and would have been a glorious sight in a telescope. I could even make out the moon beside it whenever the vapours momentarily thinned. It was now impossible to see the corpse—my only landmark—so I blundered back to the central chamber after a few false turns. After all, I would have to give up hope of sleeping on dry ground. Nothing could be done till daylight, and I might as well make the best of it here. Lying down in the mud would not be pleasant, but in my leather suit it could be done. On former expeditions I had slept under even worse conditions, and now sheer exhaustion would help to conquer repugnance.

So here I am, squatting in the slime of the central room and making these notes on my record scroll by the light of the electric lamp. There is something almost humorous in my strange, unprecedented plight. Lost in a building without doors—a building which I cannot see! I shall doubtless get out early in the morning, and ought to be back at Terra Nova with the crystal by late afternoon. It certainly is a beauty—with surprising lustre even in the feeble light of this lamp. I have just had it out examining it. Despite my fatigue, sleep is slow in coming, so I find myself writing at great length. I must stop now. Not much danger of being bothered by those cursed natives in this place. The thing I like least is the corpse—but fortunately my oxygen mask saves me from the worst effects. I am using the chlorate cubes very sparingly. Will take a couple of food tablets now and turn in. More later.

LATER—AFTERNOON, VI, 13

There has been more trouble than I expected. I am still in the building, and will have to work quickly and wisely if I expect to rest on dry ground tonight. It took me a long time to get to sleep, and I did not wake till almost noon today. As it was, I would have slept longer but for the glare of the sun through the haze. The corpse was a rather bad sight—wriggling with sificlighs, and with a cloud of farnoth-flies around it. Something had pushed the helmet away from the face, and it was better not to look at it. I was doubly glad of my oxygen mask when I thought of the situation.

At length I shook and brushed myself dry, took a couple of food tablets, and put a new potassium chlorate cube in the electrolyser of the mask. I am using these cubes slowly, but wish I had a larger supply. I felt much better after my sleep, and expected to get out of the building very shortly.

Consulting the notes and sketches I had jotted down, I was impressed by the complexity of the hallways, and by the possibility that I had made a fundamental error. Of the six openings leading out of the central space, I had chosen a certain one as that by which I had entered—using a sighting-arrangement as a guide. When I stood just within the opening, the corpse fifty yards away was exactly in line with a particular lepidodendron in the far-off forest. Now it occurred to me that this sighting might not have been of sufficient accuracy—the distance of the corpse making its difference of direction in relation to the horizon comparatively slight when viewed from the openings next to that of my first ingress. Moreover, the tree did not differ as distinctly as it might from other lepidodendra on the horizon.

Putting the matter to a test, I found to my chagrin that I could not be sure which of three openings was the right one. Had I traversed a different set of windings at each attempted exit? This time I would be sure. It struck me that despite the impossibility of trailblazing there was one marker I could leave. Though I could not spare my suit, I could—because of my thick head of hair—spare my helmet; and this was large and light enough to remain visible above the thin mud. Accordingly I removed the roughly hemispherical device and laid it at the entrance of one of the corridors—the right-hand one of the three I must try.

I would follow this corridor on the assumption that it was correct; repeating what I seemed to recall as the proper turns, and constantly consulting and making notes. If I did not get out, I would systematically exhaust all possible variations; and if these failed, I would proceed to cover the avenues extending from the next opening in the same way—continuing to the third opening if necessary. Sooner or later I could not avoid hitting the right path to the exit, but I must use patience. Even at worst, I could scarcely fail to reach the open plain in time for a dry night's sleep.

Immediate results were rather discouraging, though they helped me eliminate the right-hand opening in little more than an hour. Only a succession of blind alleys, each ending at a great distance from the corpse, seemed to branch from this hallway; and I saw very soon that it had not figured at all in the previous afternoon's wanderings. As before, however, I always found it relatively easy to grope back to the central chamber.

About 1 p.m. I shifted my helmet marker to the next opening and began to explore the hallways beyond it. At first I thought I recognised the turnings, but soon found myself in a wholly unfamiliar set of corridors. I could not get near the corpse, and this time seemed cut off from the central chamber as well, even though I thought I had recorded every move I made. There seemed to be tricky twists and crossings too subtle for me to capture in my crude diagrams, and I began to develop a kind of mixed anger and discouragement. While patience would of course win in the end, I saw that my searching would have to be minute, tireless, and long-continued.

Two o'clock found me still wandering vainly through strange corridors—constantly feeling my way, looking alternately at my helmet and at the corpse, and jotting data on my scroll with decreasing confidence. I cursed the stupidity and idle curiosity which had drawn me into this tangle of unseen walls—reflecting that if I had let the thing alone and headed back as soon as I had taken the crystal from the body, I would even now be safe at Terra Nova.

Suddenly it occurred to me that I might be able to tunnel under the invisible walls with my knife, and thus effect a short cut to the outside—or to some outward-leading corridor. I had no means of knowing how deep the building's foundations were, but the omnipresent mud argued the absence of any floor save the earth. Facing the distant and increasingly horrible corpse, I began a course of feverish digging with the broad, sharp blade.

There was about six inches of semi-liquid mud, below which the density of the soil increased sharply. This lower soil seemed to be of a different colour—a greyish clay rather like the formations near Venus's north pole. As I continued downward close to the unseen barrier I saw that the ground was getting harder and harder. Watery mud rushed into the excavation as fast as I removed the clay, but I reached through it and kept on working. If I could bore any kind of a passage beneath the wall, the mud would not stop my wriggling out.

About three feet down, however, the hardness of the soil halted my digging seriously. Its tenacity was beyond anything I had encountered before, even on this planet, and was linked with an anomalous heaviness. My knife had to split and chip the tightly packed clay, and the fragments I brought up were like solid stones or bits of metal. Finally even this splitting and chipping became impossible, and I had to cease my work with no lower edge of wall in reach.

The hour-long attempt was a wasteful as well as futile one, for it used up great stores of my energy and forced me both to take an extra food tablet, and to put an additional chlorate cube in the oxygen mask. It has also brought a pause in the day's gropings, for I am still much too exhausted to walk. After cleaning my hands and arms of the worst of the mud I sat down to write these notes—leaning against an invisible wall and facing away from the corpse.

That body is simply a writhing mass of vermin now—the odour has begun to draw some of the slimy akmans from the far-off jungle. I notice that many of the efjeh-weeds on the plain are reaching out necrophagous feelers toward the thing; but I doubt if any are long enough to reach it. I wish some really carnivorous organisms like the skorahs would appear, for then they might scent me and wriggle a course through the building toward me. Things like that have an odd sense of direction. I could watch them as they came, and jot down their approximate route if they failed to form a continuous line. Even that would be a great help. When I met any the pistol would make short work of them.

But I can hardly hope for as much as that. Now that these notes are made I shall rest a while longer, and later will do some more groping. As soon as I get back to the central chamber—which ought to be fairly easy—I shall try the extreme left-hand opening. Perhaps I can get outside by dusk after all.

NIGHT—VI, 13

New trouble. My escape will be tremendously difficult, for there are elements I had not suspected. Another night here in the mud, and a fight on my hands tomorrow. I cut my rest short and was up and groping again by four o'clock. After about fifteen minutes I reached the central chamber and moved my helmet to mark the last of the three possible doorways. Starting through this opening, I seemed to find the going more familiar, but was brought up short in less than five minutes by a sight that jolted me more than I can describe.

It was a group of four or five of those detestable man-lizards emerging from the forest far off across the plain. I could not see them distinctly at that distance, but thought they paused and turned toward the trees to gesticulate, after which they were joined by fully a dozen more. The augmented party now began to advance directly toward the invisible building, and as they approached I studied them carefully. I had never before had a close view of the things outside the steamy shadows of the jungle.

The resemblance to reptiles was perceptible, though I knew it was only an apparent one, since these beings have no point of contact with terrestrial life. When they drew nearer they seemed less truly reptilian—only the flat head and the green, slimy, frog-like skin carrying out the idea. They walked erect on their odd, thick stumps, and their suction-discs made curious noises in the mud. These were average specimens, about seven feet in height, and with four long, ropy pectoral tentacles. The motions of those tentacles—if the theories of Fogg, Ekberg, and Janat are right, which I formerly doubted but am now more ready to believe—indicated that the things were in animated conversation.

I drew my flame pistol and was ready for a hard fight. The odds were bad, but the weapon gave me a certain advantage. If the things knew this building they would come through it after me, and in this way would form a key to getting out, just as carnivorous skorahs might have done. That they would attack me seemed certain; for even though they could not see the crystal in my pouch, they could divine its presence through that special sense of theirs.

Yet, surprisingly enough, they did not attack me. Instead they scattered and formed a vast circle around me—at a distance which indicated that they were pressing close to the unseen wall. Standing there in a ring, the beings stared silently and inquisitively at me, waving their tentacles and sometimes nodding their heads and gesturing with their upper limbs. After a while I saw others issue from the forest, and these advanced and joined the curious crowd. Those near the corpse looked briefly at it but made no move to disturb it. It was a horrible sight, yet the man-lizards seemed quite unconcerned. Now and then one of them would brush away the farnoth-flies with its limbs or tentacles, or crush a wriggling sificligh or akman, or an out-reaching efjeh-weed, with the suction discs on its stumps.

Staring back at these grotesque and unexpected intruders, and wondering uneasily why they did not attack me at once, I lost for the time being the will power and nervous energy to continue my search for a way out. Instead I leaned limply against the invisible wall of the passage where I stood, letting my wonder merge gradually into a chain of the wildest speculations. An hundred mysteries which had previously baffled me seemed all at once to take on a new and sinister significance, and I trembled with an acute fear unlike anything I had experienced before.

I believed I knew why these repulsive beings were hovering expectantly around me. I believed, too, that I had the secret of the transparent structure at last. The alluring crystal which I had seized, the body of the man who had seized it before me—all these things began to acquire a dark and threatening meaning.

It was no common series of mischances which had made me lose my way in this roofless, unseen tangle of corridors. Far from it. Beyond doubt, the place was a genuine maze—a labyrinth deliberately built by these hellish beings whose craft and mentality I had so badly underestimated. Might I not have suspected this before, knowing of their uncanny architectural skill? The purpose was all too plain. It was a trap—a trap set to catch human beings, and with the crystal spheroid as bait. These reptilian things, in their war on the takers of crystals, had turned to strategy and were using our own cupidity against us.

Dwight—if this rotting corpse were indeed he—was a victim. He must have been trapped some time ago, and had failed to find his way out. Lack of water had doubtless maddened him, and perhaps he had run out of chlorate cubes as well. Probably his mask had not slipped accidentally after all. Suicide was a likelier thing. Rather than face a lingering death he had solved the issue by removing the mask deliberately and letting the lethal atmosphere do its work at once. The horrible irony of his fate lay in his position—only a few feet from the saving exit he had failed to find. One minute more of searching and he would have been safe.

And now I was trapped as he had been. Trapped, and with this circling herd of curious starers to mock at my predicament. The thought was maddening, and as it sank in I was seized with a sudden flash of panic which set me running aimlessly through the unseen hallways. For several moments I was essentially a maniac—stumbling, tripping, bruising myself on the invisible walls, and finally collapsing in the mud as a panting, lacerated heap of mindless, bleeding flesh.

The fall sobered me a bit, so that when I slowly struggled to my feet I could notice things and exercise my reason. The circling watchers were swaying their tentacles in an odd, irregular way suggestive of sly, alien laughter, and I shook my fist savagely at them as I rose. My gesture seemed to increase their hideous mirth—a few of them clumsily imitating it with their greenish upper limbs. Shamed into sense, I tried to collect my faculties and take stock of the situation.

After all, I was not as badly off as Dwight had been. Unlike him, I knew what the situation was—and forewarned is forearmed. I had proof that the exit was attainable in the end, and would not repeat his tragic act of impatient despair. The body—or skeleton, as it would soon be—was constantly before me as a guide to the sought-for aperture, and dogged patience would certainly take me to it if I worked long and intelligently enough.

I had, however, the disadvantage of being surrounded by these reptilian devils. Now that I realised the nature of the trap—whose invisible material argued a science and technology beyond anything on earth—I could no longer discount the mentality and resources of my enemies. Even with my flame pistol I would have a bad time getting away—though boldness and quickness would doubtless see me through in the long run.

But first I must reach the exterior—unless I could lure or provoke some of the creatures to advance toward me. As I prepared my pistol for action and counted over my generous supply of ammunition it occurred to me to try the effect of its blasts on the invisible walls. Had I overlooked a feasible means of escape? There was no clue to the chemical composition of the transparent barrier, and conceivably it might be something which a tongue of fire could cut like cheese. Choosing a section facing the corpse, I carefully discharged the pistol at close range and felt with my knife where the blast had been aimed. Nothing was changed. I had seen the flame spread when it struck the surface, and now I realised that my hope had been vain. Only a long, tedious search for the exit would ever bring me to the outside.

So, swallowing another food tablet and putting another cube in the electrolyser of my mask, I recommenced the long quest; retracing my steps to the central chamber and starting out anew. I constantly consulted my notes and sketches, and made fresh ones—taking one false turn after another, but staggering on in desperation till the afternoon light grew very dim. As I persisted in my quest I looked from time to time at the silent circle of mocking starers, and noticed a gradual replacement in their ranks. Every now and then a few would return to the forest, while others would arrive to take their places. The more I thought of their tactics the less I liked them, for they gave me a hint of the creatures' possible motives. At any time these devils could have advanced and fought me, but they seemed to prefer watching my struggles to escape. I could not but infer that they enjoyed the spectacle—and this made me shrink with double force from the prospect of falling into their hands.

With the dark I ceased my searching, and sat down in the mud to rest. Now I am writing in the light of my lamp, and will soon try to get some sleep. I hope tomorrow will see me out; for my canteen is low, and lacol tablets are a poor substitute for water. I would hardly dare to try the moisture in this slime, for none of the water in the mud-regions is potable except when distilled. That is why we run such long pipe lines to the yellow clay regions—or depend on rain-water when those devils find and cut our pipes. I have none too many chlorate cubes either, and must try to cut down my oxygen consumption as much as I can. My tunnelling attempt of the early afternoon, and my later panic flight, burned up a perilous amount of air. Tomorrow I will reduce physical exertion to the barest minimum until I meet the reptiles and have to deal with them. I must have a good cube supply for the journey back to Terra Nova. My enemies are still on hand; I can see a circle of their feeble glow-torches around me. There is a horror about those lights which will keep me awake.

NIGHT—VI, 14

Another full day of searching and still no way out! I am beginning to be worried about the water problem, for my canteen went dry at noon. In the afternoon there was a burst of rain, and I went back to the central chamber for the helmet which I had left as a marker—using this as a bowl and getting about two cupfuls of water. I drank most of it, but have put the slight remainder in my canteen. Lacol tablets make little headway against real thirst, and I hope there will be more rain in the night. I am leaving my helmet bottom up to catch any that falls. Food tablets are none too plentiful, but not dangerously low. I shall halve my rations from now on. The chlorate cubes are my real worry, for even without violent exercise the day's endless tramping burned a dangerous number. I feel weak from my forced economies in oxygen, and from my constantly mounting thirst. When I reduce my food I suppose I shall feel still weaker.

There is something damnable—something uncanny—about this labyrinth. I could swear that I had eliminated certain turns through charting, and yet each new trial belies some assumption I had thought established. Never before did I realise how lost we are without visual landmarks. A blind man might do better— but for most of us sight is the king of the senses. The effect of all these fruitless wanderings is one of profound discouragement. I can understand how poor Dwight must have felt. His corpse is now just a skeleton, and the sificlighs and akmans and farnoth-flies are gone. The efjeh-weeds are nipping the leather clothing to pieces, for they were longer and faster-growing than I had expected. And all the while those relays of tentacled starers stand gloatingly around the barrier laughing at me and enjoying my misery. Another day and I shall go mad if I do not drop dead from exhaustion.

However, there is nothing to do but persevere. Dwight would have got out if he had kept on a minute longer. It is just possible that somebody from Terra Nova will come looking for me before long, although this is only my third day out. My muscles ache horribly, and I can't seem to rest at all lying down in this loathsome mud. Last night, despite my terrific fatigue, I slept only fitfully, and tonight I fear will be no better. I live in an endless nightmare—poised between waking and sleeping, yet neither truly awake nor truly asleep. My hand shakes, I can write no more for the time being. That circle of feeble glow-torches is hideous.

LATE AFTERNOON—VI, 15

Substantial progress! Looks good. Very weak, and did not sleep much till daylight. Then I dozed till noon, though without being at all rested. No rain, and thirst leaves me very weak. Ate an extra food tablet to keep me going, but without water it didn't help much. I dared to try a little of the slime water just once, but it made me violently sick and left me even thirstier than before. Must save chlorate cubes, so am nearly suffocating for lack of oxygen. Can't walk much of the time, but manage to crawl in the mud. About 2 p.m. I thought I recognised some passages, and got substantially nearer to the corpse—or skeleton—than I had been since the first day's trials. I was sidetracked once in a blind alley, but recovered the main trail with the aid of my chart and notes. The trouble with these jottings is that there are so many of them. They must cover three feet of the record scroll, and I have to stop for long periods to untangle them.

My head is weak from thirst, suffocation, and exhaustion, and I cannot understand all I have set down. Those damnable green things keep staring and laughing with their tentacles, and sometimes they gesticulate in a way that makes me think they share some terrible joke just beyond my perception.

It was three o'clock when I really struck my stride. There was a doorway which, according to my notes, I had not traversed before; and when I tried it I found I could crawl circuitously toward the weed-twined skeleton. The route was a sort of spiral, much like that by which I had first reached the central chamber. Whenever I came to a lateral doorway or junction I would keep to the course which seemed best to repeat that original journey. As I circled nearer and nearer to my gruesome landmark, the watchers outside intensified their cryptic gesticulations and sardonic silent laughter. Evidently they saw something grimly amusing in my progress—perceiving no doubt how helpless I would be in any encounter with them. I was content to leave them to their mirth; for although I realised my extreme weakness, I counted on the flame pistol and its numerous extra magazines to get me through the vile reptilian phalanx.

Hope now soared high, but I did not attempt to rise to my feet. Better to crawl now, and save my strength for the coming encounter with the man-lizards. My advance was very slow, and the danger of straying into some blind alley very great, but none the less I seemed to curve steadily toward my osseous goal. The prospect gave me new strength, and for the nonce I ceased to worry about my pain, my thirst, and my scant supply of cubes. The creatures were now all massing around the entrance—gesturing, leaping, and laughing with their tentacles. Soon, I reflected, I would have to face the entire horde—and perhaps such reinforcements as they would receive from the forest.

I am now only a few yards from the skeleton, and am pausing to make this entry before emerging and breaking through the noxious band of entities. I feel confident that with my last ounce of strength I can put them to flight despite their numbers, for the range of this pistol is tremendous. Then a camp on the dry moss at the plateau's edge, and in the morning a weary trip through the jungle to Terra Nova. I shall be glad to see living men and the buildings of human beings again. The teeth of that skull gleam and grin horribly.

TOWARD NIGHT—VI, 15

Horror and despair. Baffled again! After making the previous entry I approached still closer to the skeleton, but suddenly encountered an intervening wall. I had been deceived once more, and was apparently back where I had been three days before, on my first futile attempt to leave the labyrinth Whether I screamed aloud I do not know—perhaps I was too weak to utter a sound. I merely lay dazed in the mud for a long period, while the greenish things outside leaped and laughed and gestured.

After a time I became more fully conscious. My thirst and

weakness and suffocation were fast gaining on me, and with my last bit of strength I put a new cube in the electrolyser—recklessly, and without regard for the needs of my journey to Terra Nova. The fresh oxygen revived me slightly, and enabled me to look about more alertly.

It seemed as if I were slightly more distant from poor Dwight than I had been at that first disappointment, and I dully wondered if I could be in some other corridor a trifle more remote. With this faint shadow of hope I laboriously dragged myself forward—but after a few feet encountered a dead end as I had on the former occasion.

This, then, was the end. Three days had taken me nowhere, and my strength was gone. I would soon go mad from thirst, and I could no longer count on cubes enough to get me back. I feebly wondered why the nightmare things had gathered so thickly around the entrance as they mocked me. Probably this was part of the mockery—to make me think I was approaching an egress which they knew did not exist.

I shall not last long, though I am resolved not to hasten matters as Dwight did. His grinning skull has just turned toward me, shifted by the groping of one of the efjeh-weeds that are devouring his leather suit. The ghoulish stare of those empty eye-sockets is worse than the staring of those lizard horrors. It lends a hideous meaning to that dead, white-toothed grin.

I shall lie very still in the mud and save all the strength I can. This record—which I hope may reach and warn those who come after me—will soon be done. After I stop writing I shall rest a long while. Then, when it is too dark for those frightful creatures to see, I shall muster up my last reserves of strength and try to toss the record scroll over the wall and the intervening corridor to the plain outside. I shall take care to send it toward the left, where it will not hit the leaping band of mocking beleaguerers. Perhaps it will be lost forever in the thin mud—but perhaps it will land in some widespread clump of weeds and ultimately reach the hands of men.

If it does survive to be read, I hope it may do more than merely warn men of this trap. I hope it may teach our race to let those shining crystals stay where they are. They belong to Venus alone. Our planet does not truly need them, and I believe we have violated some obscure and mysterious law—some law buried deep in the arcana of the cosmos—in our attempts to take them. Who can tell what dark, potent, and widespread forces spur on these reptilian things who guard their treasure so strangely? Dwight and I have paid, as others have paid and will pay. But it may be that these scattered deaths are only the prelude of greater horrors to come. Let us leave to Venus that which belongs only to Venus.

* * * * *

I am very near death now, and fear I may not be able to throw the scroll when dusk comes. If I cannot, I suppose the man-lizards will seize it, for they will probably realise what it is. They will not wish anyone to be warned of the labyrinth—and they will not know that my message holds a plea in their own behalf. As the end approaches I feel more kindly toward the things. In the scale of cosmic entity who can say which species stands higher, or more nearly approaches a space-wide organic norm—theirs or mine?

* * * * *

I have just taken the great crystal out of my pouch to look at in my last moments. It shines fiercely and menacingly in the red rays of the dying day. The leaping horde have noticed it, and their gestures have changed in a way I cannot understand. I wonder why they keep clustered around the entrance instead of concentrating at a still closer point in the transparent wall.

* * * * *

I am growing numb and cannot write much more. Things whirl around me, yet I do not lose consciousness. Can I throw this over the wall? That crystal glows so, yet the twilight is deepening.

* * * * *

Dark. Very weak. They are still laughing and leaping around the doorway, and have started those hellish glow-torches.

* * * * *

Are they going away? I dreamed I heard a sound . . . light in the sky.

REPORT OF WESLEY P. MILLER, SUPT. GROUP A,

VENUS CRYSTAL CO.

(Terra Nova on Venus—VI, 16)

Our Operative A-49, Kenton J. Stanfield of 5317 Marshall Street, Richmond, Va., left Terra Nova early on VI, 12, for a short-term trip indicated by detector. Due back 13th or 14th. Did not appear by evening of 15th, so Scouting Plane FR-58 with five men under my command set out at 8 p.m. to follow route with detector. Needle shewed no change from earlier readings.

Followed needle to Erycinian Highland, played strong searchlights all the way. Triple-range flame-guns and D-radiation-cylinders could have dispersed any ordinary hostile force of natives, or any dangerous aggregation of carnivorous skorahs.

When over the open plain on Eryx we saw a group of

moving lights which we knew were native glow-torches. As we approached, they scattered into the forest. Probably 75 to 100 in all. Detector indicated crystal on spot where they had been. Sailing low over this spot, our lights picked out objects on the ground. Skeleton tangled in efjeh-weeds, and complete body ten feet from it. Brought plane down near bodies, and corner of wing crashed on unseen obstruction.

Approaching bodies on foot, we came up short against a smooth, invisible barrier which puzzled us enormously. Feeling along it near the skeleton, we struck an opening, beyond which was a space with another opening leading to the skeleton. The latter, though robbed of clothing by weeds, had one of the company's numbered metal helmets beside it. It was Operative B-9, Frederick N. Dwight of Koenig's division, who had been out of Terra Nova for two months on a long commission.

Between this skeleton and the complete body there seemed to be another wall, but we could easily identify the second man as Stanfield. He had a record scroll in his left hand and a pen in his right, and seemed to have been writing when he died. No crystal was visible, but the detector indicated a huge specimen near Stanfield's body.

We had great difficulty in getting at Stanfield, but finally succeeded. The body was still warm, and a great crystal lay beside it, covered by the shallow mud. We at once studied the record scroll in the left hand, and prepared to take certain steps based on its data. The contents of the scroll forms the long narrative prefixed to this report; a narrative whose main descriptions we have verified, and which we append as an explanation of what was found. The later parts of this account shew mental decay, but there is no reason to doubt the bulk of it. Stanfield obviously died of a combination of thirst, suffocation, cardiac strain, and psychological depression. His mask was in place, and freely generating oxygen despite an alarmingly low cube supply.

Our plane being damaged, we sent a wireless and called out Anderson with Repair Plane FG-7, a crew of wreckers, and a set of blasting materials. By morning FR-58 was fixed, and went back under Anderson carrying the two bodies and the crystal. We shall bury Dwight and Stanfield in the company graveyard, and ship the crystal to Chicago on the next earth-bound liner. Later, we shall adopt Stanfield's suggestion—the sound one in the saner, earlier part of his report—and bring across enough troops to wipe out the natives altogether. With a clear field, there can be scarcely any limit to the amount of crystal we can secure.

In the afternoon we studied the invisible building or trap with great care, exploring it with the aid of long guiding cords, and preparing a complete chart for our archives. We were much impressed by the design, and shall keep specimens of the substance for chemical analysis. All such knowledge will be useful when we take over the various cities of the natives. Our type C diamond drills were able to bite into the unseen material, and wreckers are now planting dynamite preparatory to a thorough blasting. Nothing will be left when we are done. The edifice forms a distinct menace to aërial and other possible traffic.

In considering the plan of the labyrinth one is impressed not only with the irony of Dwight's fate, but with that of Stanfield's as well. When trying to reach the second body from the skeleton, we could find no access on the right, but Markheim found a doorway from the first inner space some fifteen feet past Dwight and four or five past Stanfield. Beyond this was a long hall which we did not explore till later, but on the right-hand side of that hall was another doorway leading directly to the body. Stanfield could have reached the outside entrance by walking 22 or 23 feet if he had found the opening which lay directly behind him—an opening which he overlooked in his exhaustion and despair.